ANDREW'S TRIP

TO THE GROCERY STORE

PRINTED IN THE UNITED STATES OF AMERICA

FIRST PRINTING, 2024

ISBN: 9798876627278

INDEPENDENT PUBLISHING

697 TILLMAN ROAD

RIDGELAND, SC 29936

WRITTEN AND ILLUSTRATED BY: ROXANNE WILLIAMS

ANDREW'S TRIP

TO THE GROCERY STORE

DEDICATION

Bug,

You are my inspiration in so many ways. Your smile, curious nature, contagious laughter, and endless amounts of energy make everyone love you. You are smart beyond your years and there isn't anyone else like you in the whole world! Whenever you need a reminder of just how amazing you are, read this book and remember that I love you and I will forever be thankful to have been your Chachee!

I Love You Always,

Chachee

Once upon a time, in a cozy little town,
Lived a boy named Andrew, who often
wore a worried frown.
With his heart in a fluster and his mind
filled with fears,
Just going to the grocery store would
bring him to tears.

He feared the monsters hiding in
between aisles,
Of the creatures lurking with their
fang-filled smiles.
Each minute he waited, his anxiety
grew stronger,
He didn't know if he could take this
much longer.

His thoughts had his head filled with misinformation, But he can conquer these fears with his BIG imagination! With a heart full of courage and eyes full of glee, Andrew decided to turn the grocery store into a circus, you see.

When he stepped through the door, the world changed all around,
The produce section worker became a hilarious clown.
The fruits he began juggling and the vegetables he stacked,
Andrew's worries started fading, and his frown soon had cracked.

The cereal aisle narrowed into a tightrope
walk,
And Andrew, with newfound confidence,
started to stalk.
One foot in front of the other,
this was a breeze.
He passed the cinnamon cereal, Oh no, try
not to sneeze!
He was a trapeze artist, walking oh so high,
Conquering his fears and reaching for the
sky!

Off to the milk which turned into a carousel,
With different flavors as horses, apes, and gazelles.
Strawberry, chocolate, and just plain white,
All were lined up ready to take flight!
Andrew hopped on a pink pony, fearlessly taking a ride,
His worries slipped away with every passing stride.

The bakery department became a magic show,
With breadsticks becoming wands, from which rainbows would flow.
Andrew, with his imagination, became the magician ring leader,
His confidence grew with cheers from his biggest cheerleader.

As he ventured through each aisle, in this circus made of dreams,
Andrew realized that his fears were not as they seemed.
He laughed with the dancing vegetables and sang with the cashier,
His creativity conquered his anxieties leaving nothing to fear.

Andrew conquered his fear of the
grocery store today,
With courage, bravery, and
imaginative play.
His fears were quite silly upon further
inspection,
For each fear that he conquers his
anxiety of new places lessened.

So, if you spot a child like Andrew when you're at the store,
Remember, they're not misbehaving or trying to be a chore.
They just require your understanding, patience, and love.
To conquer their fears and to rise above.

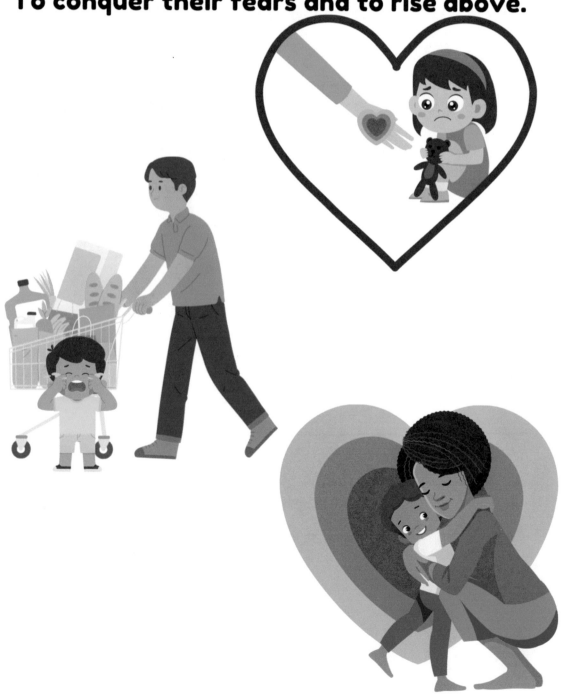

Help bring laughter to their heart and dry up their tears,
Join in their imaginary land that squashes their fears.
Help battle dragons, be silly, or sing songs.
For they won't be little or fearful for too long.

And the next time you feel anxious and your worries run amok,
Remember Andrew's story, and give your imagination a little luck.
For within the realms of creativity lies new frontiers,
You too can find the strength to conquer those fears.

THE END

Andrew's Adventures that are currently available on Amazon and select stores:

Andrew's Trip to the Dentist

Be on the lookout for:

Andrew's Trip to the Optomitrist

Andrew's Trip to the Party

Andrew's Trip to the Carwash

ABOUT THE AUTHOR

ROXANNE WILLIAMS

SHARES HER LIFE WITH FIVE
WONDERFUL BOYS AND HER PARTNER,
MICHAEL. TOGETHER THEY ENJOY
WATCHING THE BOYS PLAY SPORTS,
TRAVELING, FISHING, CARS, AND BEING
OUTDOORS. SHE HAS SPENT MOST OF
HER ADULT LIFE TEACHING CHILDREN.
IT HAS ALWAYS BEEN HER DREAM TO
CREATE STORIES THAT ENCOURAGE
CHILDREN'S IMAGINATION WHILE
HELPING TEACH TOUGH LESSONS.

THANK YOU FOR BEING A PART OF
THAT DREAM.

Made in the USA
Columbia, SC
05 April 2024

33784082R10015